The Foolish, Timid Rabbit

Written by Lou Kuenzler

Illustrated by Beatrice Bencivenni

Collins

There was a crash. Thumper shook with fear.

He ran to tell Buck.

"Did you hear that crash?"
said Thumper. "I think the planet
will crack!"

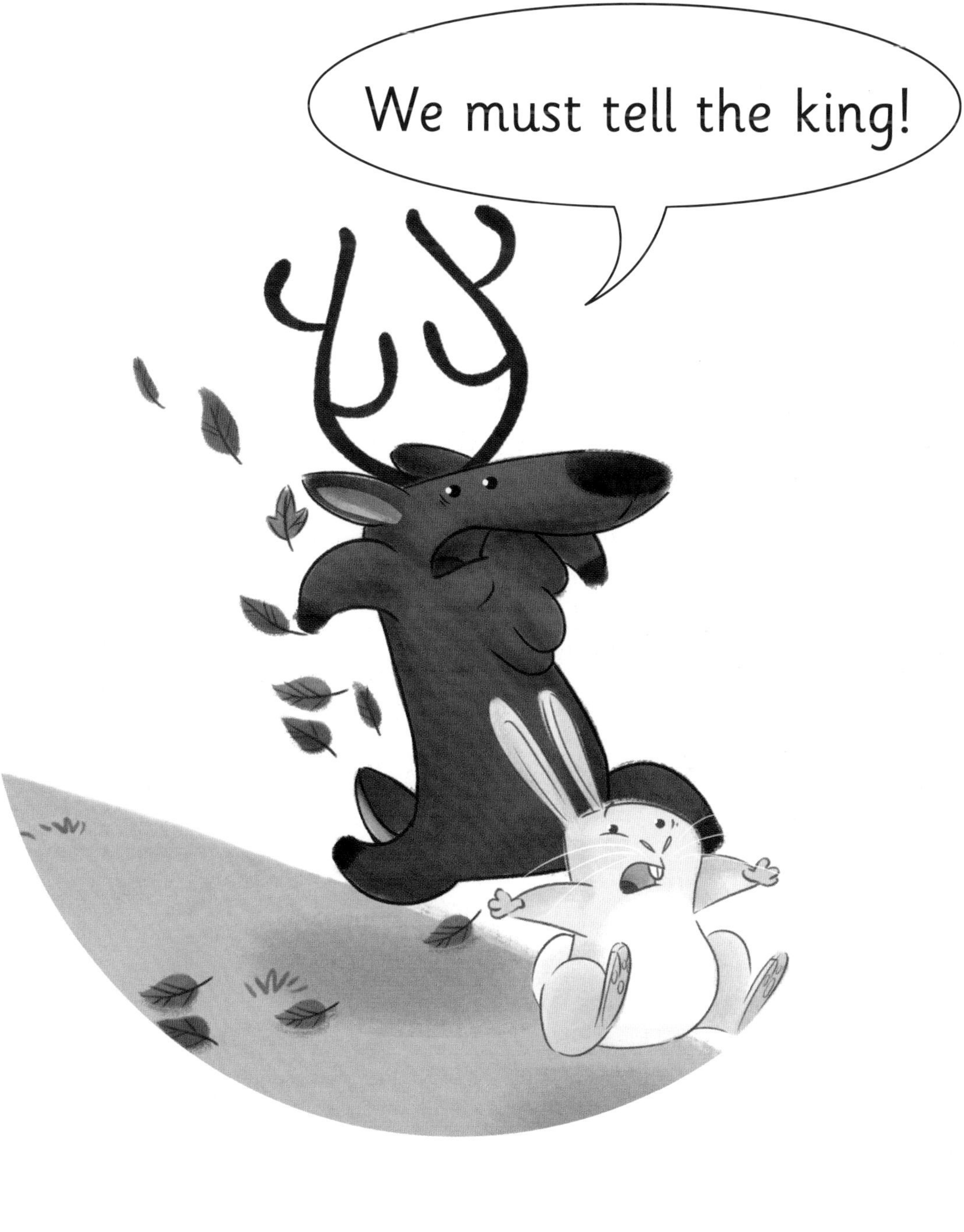
We must tell the king!

They ran by Vixen.

The planet will split.

We must tell the king.

The pals sped by Tusker.

The planet will snap apart.

8

"Stop!" said the king.
"What is the matter?"

"Did you hear that crash?"
Thumper said.

The king said, "Look. It was just a nut!"

11

Then Thumper went red.

"We can stop," he said. "The planet will not crack!"

Will the planet crack?

After reading

Letters and Sounds: Phase 4

Word count: 99

Focus on adjacent consonants with short vowel phonemes, e.g. /c/ /r/ /a/ /sh/

Common exception words: to, the, I, by, he, we, was, you, they, there, said, what

Curriculum links (EYFS): Understanding the World: The World

Curriculum links (National Curriculum, Year 1): Geography

Early learning goals: Listening and attention: children listen to stories, accurately anticipating key events and respond to what they hear with relevant comments, questions or actions; Understanding: answer 'how' and 'why' questions about their experiences and in response to stories or events; Reading: read and understand simple sentences, use phonic knowledge to decode regular words and read them aloud accurately, read some common irregular words

National Curriculum learning objectives: Spoken language: listen and respond appropriately to adults and their peers; Reading/word reading: apply phonic knowledge and skills as the route to decode words, read aloud accurately books that are consistent with their developing phonic knowledge and that do not require them to use other strategies to work out words; Reading/comprehension: develop pleasure in reading, motivation to read, vocabulary and understanding by making inferences on the basis of what is being said and done

Developing fluency

- Your child may enjoy hearing you read the book.
- Model reading the speech bubbles and dialogue with expression.
- Have fun reading the book together, with you reading the main text and your child reading the speech bubbles.

Phonic practice

- Practise reading words that contain adjacent consonants. Model sounding out the following word, saying each of the sounds quickly and clearly. Then blend the sounds together.

  c/r/a/sh

- Ask your child to find another word that starts with the two letters **c** and **r** on page 4. (*crack*)
- Look at page 6 together. Ask your child to sound out the words **planet** and **split**.